Text copyright © Leon Rosselson 1998
Illustrations copyright © Nick Ward 1998

First published in Great Britain in 1998
by Macdonald Young Books
an imprint of Wayland Publishers Ltd
61 Western Road
Hove
East Sussex
BN3 1JD
Find Macdonald Young Books on the internet at
http://www.myb.co.uk

Designed and Typeset by Backup Creative Service, Dorset DT10 1DB
Printed and bound in Belgium by Proost International Book Production

British Library Cataloguing in Publication Data available

ISBN 0 7500 2537 9

Leon Rosselson

Carla's Magic Dancing Boots

Illustrated by Nick Ward

Chapter One

She loved them. They were half-price in a sale and a perfect fit. Her feet felt as if they belonged in those boots. And best of all, they were golden. Golden boots. They seemed to sparkle in the sun.

"What lovely boots," her mother said. "I wouldn't mind a pair like that myself."

Carla couldn't wait to show them off to her schoolfriends, Lauren and Yasmin. On Monday morning, she danced ahead of her mother all the way to school. She ran up to Lauren and Yasmin when she saw they were already in the playground.

"I've got new boots," she announced proudly.

Her friends were both wearing shiny black patent leather shoes with silver buckles and heavy heels.

Lauren looked at Carla's new golden boots and laughed. "They're horrible," she said. "They're stupid."

Carla was shocked. "They're not," she replied. "They were half-price in a sale."

"Course they were," Yasmin said. "Who'd want to buy boots like that?"

Carla turned away, tears filling her eyes. "I hate you," she said.

"We don't care," said Lauren. "We don't want to be friends with old silly boots anyway."

And they marched off, their noses in the air, their heavy heels clattering on the playground.

All that week, Carla's friends Lauren and Yasmin were not being her friends. Whenever they passed her, they would call out, "Silly boots! Silly boots!"

Chapter Two

On Saturday, Carla went to stay with her grandmother for the day. She was wearing her golden boots. There was a delicious smell of baking in the kitchen.

"It's lovely to see you, Carla," her grandmother said. "I'm making some biscuits. They should be ready soon if you'd like one."

"Yes, please," said Carla. She loved her grandmother's biscuits.

"How's school?" asked her grandmother.

"Horrible," Carla said. "Lauren and Yasmin aren't talking to me."

"Oh. Why is that then?"

"Because of my new boots," Carla said.

"Your boots? But they're lovely boots."

Carla shook her head. "Lauren and Yasmin say they're stupid."

Her grandmother looked at Carla's sad face and bent down to give her a kiss.

"Maybe," she said, "maybe Lauren and Yasmin don't know they're magic boots."

Carla looked down at her golden boots, a puzzled expression on her face. "What do you mean, Grandma?"

"It's as clear as day," Grandma said. "They're magic boots. I knew it as soon as I saw them."

"How are they magic, Grandma?"

"How? They dance. That's how."

Carla looked unsure. "I've never seen them dance," she said.

"Well, of course," Grandma said.
"Because you haven't recited the magic
words yet, have you?"

"What magic words?"

"I'll show you," said Grandma. "Come
with me."

Chapter Three

Carla followed Grandma into the
living-room. "Let's clear a space here,"
Grandma said as she pushed the
armchairs to one side.

"You're not going to dance now,
Grandma?" Carla asked, rather alarmed.

"I certainly am," Grandma said.

"But you can't."

"And why not, pray?"

"You're too old," Carla said.

"There's no such thing as being too old to dance, Carla," her grandmother said. "Now you just pay attention."

Her grandmother threw off her apron, clapped her hands and started chanting.

"Ma-gic boots, ma-gic boots, you can dance like this with ma-gic boots."
And as she chanted, she began to sway from side to side and then, holding her dress out, to move her feet in time to the chanting. A shuffle to the left, a shuffle to the right, two little skips then turn around, all the time chanting:

"If you wear them light,
If you wear them right,
You can dance all day,
You can dance all night.
You can dance the sun,
You can dance the stars,
You can dance to the moon,
You can dance to Mars.

You can dance in a ring,
You can dance in a line,
With your ma-gic boots,
With your ma-gic boots,
You can dance —
Just fine."

Carla watched in amazement as her grandmother danced faster and faster. She lifted her knees up high, flung her arms out and whirled around, until, at the end, she gave a little curtsy and collapsed into a chair, panting heavily.

Carla clapped her hands. "Can I do that, Grandma? Can I?"

"Of course, you can, Carla. Just give me a bit of time to recover and I'll teach you the magic words."

Chapter Four

When her grandmother had caught her breath again, she said, "Just copy me, Carla. First you have to tell your magic boots to get ready to dance. So clap your hands and say the magic words. Ma-gic boots, ma-gic boots, you can dance like this with ma-gic boots. Now just listen to the beat and let your magic boots take you dancing."

Carla tried to follow what her
grandmother was doing: a shuffle to the
left, a shuffle to the right, two little skips
then turn around. And she tried to recite
the magic chant. "If you wear them light,
if you wear them right…"

The first time
through, she
thought she'd
never get it right.
So they did it
again. And then
again. And again.
Now Carla was
moving with
more confidence
and even putting
her own steps in,
and the words
were coming
more easily to
her lips.

"You can dance in a ring,
You can dance in a line,
With your magic boots,
With your magic boots,
You can dance —
Just fine."
Carla gave a little curtsy.

"Well done, Carla," her grandmother said. "But I've got no breath left. I'm ready for a cup of tea and a biscuit."

Just before her father came to collect Carla and take her home, her grandmother made her recite the magic words again to make sure she hadn't forgotten them.

"And if they make fun of your boots again," Grandma said, "you just show them they're magic boots."

"Suppose they don't believe me?" Carla said.

"Don't argue with them," said her grandmother. "Let your feet do the talking."

"Let your feet do the talking," Carla muttered to herself over and over again in the car home until her father ordered her to stop because it was driving him mad.

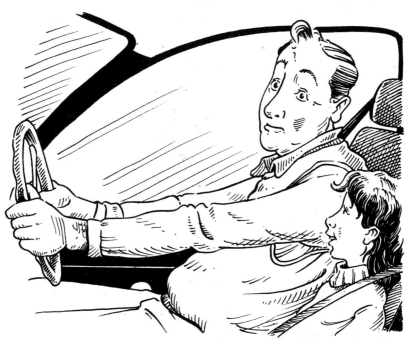

Chapter Five

The next day, straight after breakfast,
Carla went up to her room. Her mother
and father, who were sitting reading the
Sunday paper, heard strange chanting
sounds and tapping noises coming
through the ceiling.

"What *is* she doing up there?" her
mother said.

"Whatever it is," her father said, without taking his eyes off the paper, "I expect she'll grow out of it."

That was his answer for everything.

Carla's mother went upstairs to find out what Carla was doing.

"I'm dancing," Carla explained. "I can't help it," she said. "I just can't help it."

"Well," her mum said, "I never knew you were so keen on dancing."

"It's my boots," Carla said. "They're magic boots. Grandma said so."

"That explains it," her mum said smiling. "Grandma knows about these things, doesn't she?"

At school the next day, Carla was still wearing her golden boots and her friends, Lauren and Yasmin, still weren't being her friends.

Miss Wright, their class teacher, had an announcement to make about the end of the year concert. "I know some of you are going to be singing in the choir," she said, "and some of you will be playing recorders and other instruments. But if you're not doing anything and would like to take part, sing a song or recite a poem or —"

Carla's hand shot up.

"Yes, Carla?"

"Dance, Miss? Can I do a dance?"

"Well, yes. I was going to say, if you'd like to take part, come and see me at the lunch break tomorrow. OK, Carla?"

In the playground at break time, Lauren and Yasmin cornered Carla.

"You can't dance," Lauren said.

"I can so," Carla said.

"I've never seen you dance," Yasmin said.

"I've never had magic boots before," Carla said. "That's why."

"Those stupid boots aren't magic," Lauren said scornfully.

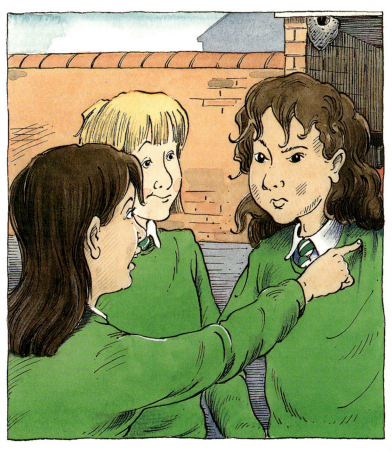

"Let your feet do the talking," Carla said under her breath. She began to sway from side to side and clap her hands in time to the chant: "Ma-gic boots, ma-gic boots —"

"She's mad," Lauren said.

But they watched silently as, still chanting the magic words, Carla shuffled and skipped and twirled and whirled, tapping her toes, wiggling her hips, throwing her arms out and lifting her knees up high.

Backwards and forwards and round and round went her magic boots sparkling golden in the sun. Carla shut her eyes and let her body and feet move to the beat of the chant and the magic of her dancing boots.

"You can dance the sun,
You can dance the stars,
You can dance to the moon,
You can dance to Mars.

"You can dance in a ring,
You can dance in a line,
With your ma-gic boots,
With your ma-gic boots,
You can dance —
Just fine."

Carla did the splits, touched the ground, pushed herself up and gave a little curtsy.

A small crowd of children who had come to watch, gave her a cheer.

Carla looked at her boots, shyly. Lauren and Yasmin whispered to each other. Then Lauren said, "If you teach us that dance, Carla, we'll be your friends again."

"You have to know the magic words as well," Carla said.

"All right, teach us them as well," Yasmin said.

Carla shook her head. "You need magic boots," she said. "You can't dance in those shoes. You'll fall down."

"We'll be your friends," Yasmin begged.

"If we all have the same magic boots," Carla said, "we can all do the dance at the school concert. They've still got the sale on at the shoe shop."

Chapter Six

The next day, Lauren and Yasmin came to school in golden boots, just like Carla's. Carla taught them the words and the dance before the bell rang for the beginning of school. They practised it again at the morning break. And at the lunch break, Miss Wright agreed to give them a spot in the concert which was a fortnight away.

They practised at Carla's house. And when Carla's mother said she couldn't stand it any more, they practised at Yasmin's house. And when Yasmin's mother said she couldn't stand it any more, they practised at Lauren's house.

And when Lauren's mother said she couldn't stand it any more, they went back to Carla's house. They added new steps. They danced side by side. They danced one behind the other. They danced round and round. They just couldn't stop dancing.

The evening of the concert arrived. The hall was full to bursting. Carla's mother, father and grandmother were in the front row. Carla was so nervous she thought she'd be sick. Her stomach felt heavy. Her knees felt wobbly. Her feet felt as if they didn't belong to her. She wouldn't be able to walk, let alone dance.

Miss Wright made the announcement.
"Now we've got a special treat for you.
Carla, Yasmin and Lauren have made up
their own dance which they're going to
perform for the first time at this concert.
So here they are. Will you please welcome
The Talking Feet."

Carla led the way on stage. She was trying to stop her knees from shaking. Yasmin and Lauren tried to smile but she could see that they were as nervous as she was. They stood in a line and swayed from side to side, clapping out the beat:

"Ma-gic boots, ma-gic boots, you can dance like this with ma-gic boots."

And it *was* like magic. As soon as she started dancing, Carla's nervousness disappeared. She felt strong and full of energy. She forgot her parents and grandmother in the front row. She forgot the audience altogether. She skipped and

shuffled and twirled and whirled and wiggled her hips and tapped her toes. She let her feet do the talking and her boots do the dancing. The three girls wove dancing patterns on the stage, their magic boots sparkling golden in the spotlights.

"You can dance in a ring;
You can dance in a line,
With your ma-gic boots,
With your ma-gic boots,
You can dance —
Just fine."

There was a burst of applause. Carla,
Yasmin and Lauren stood there, blinking.
It was over. So quickly. They wanted to
do it all over again. For the first time,
Carla became aware of the audience.

She saw her father and mother in the front row, smiling and clapping. She saw her grandmother standing up and giving her a thumbs-up sign. Instead of running into the wings as she'd been told to do, Carla jumped off the stage, danced up to her grandmother and gave her a big long hug.

"You were right, Grandma," Carla whispered. "They *are* magic boots."

"Not as magic as you are," Grandma said, beaming happily.